KV-192-525

USING THIS BOOK

*Children learn to read by **reading**, but they need help to begin with.*

When you have read the story on the left-hand pages aloud to the child, go back to the beginning of the book and look at the pictures together.

Encourage children to read the sentences under the pictures. If they don't know a word, give them a chance to 'guess' what it is from the illustrations, before telling them.

There are more suggestions for helping children to learn to read in the *Parent/Teacher* booklet.

British Library Cataloguing in Publication Data
McCullagh, Sheila K.
 The Tidy Bird. – (Puddle Lane. Stage 2; 6)
 1. Readers – 1950-
 I. Title   II. Aitchison, Martin   III. Series
 428.6   PZ7
 ISBN 0-7214-0971-7

First edition

Published by Ladybird Books Ltd Loughborough Leicestershire UK
Ladybird Books Inc Lewiston Maine 04240 USA

The Tidy Bird

written by SHEILA McCULLAGH
illustrated by MARTIN AITCHISON

This book belongs to:

Ladybird Books

One day, Sarah and Gita
were playing in Puddle Lane
when Mr Gotobed opened
the front door of his house,
and looked out.
"Have you seen my spectacles
anywhere?" he asked them.

"No," said Sarah.
"Aren't they in your house?"

"I don't think so," said Mr Gotobed.
"But it's very difficult to see them,
when I haven't got them on."

"Can we come in and help you
to look for them?" asked Gita.

Mr Gotobed
looked out of his house.

"Would you look in the garden
for me?" said Mr Gotobed.
"I was in there yesterday.
I had a little nap under a tree,
and when I woke up,
it was dark.
So I came straight home."

"We'll go and look now,"
said Sarah.
Then Mrs Pitter-Patter
came up the lane.

Mrs Pitter-Patter
came up the lane.

"Good morning, Mr Gotobed,"
said Mrs Pitter-Patter.
"Have you seen my red feather
anywhere?"

"Red feather?" asked Mr Gotobed.
He sounded very puzzled.

"Yes — the red feather I wear
in my hat," said Mrs Pitter-Patter.
She turned to Sarah and Gita.
"You haven't been playing with it,
have you?"

Mrs Pitter-Patter said,
''Have you seen
my red feather?''

Sarah and Gita had
only time to shake their heads,
when Mr Puffle came
up the lane with Davy.
"'Morning, Mrs Pitter-Patter.
'Morning, Mr Gotobed,"
Mr Puffle said cheerfully.
"You haven't seen my paint-brush,
have you? I was painting
my window-box, and I put it down
somewhere in the lane."

"I've been looking in the lane,"
said Davy. "But it's not there."

Davy and Mr Puffle
came up the lane.

"I haven't seen it,"
said Mrs Pitter-Patter.
"And I've lost my red feather.
Someone must have taken it."
She looked very hard at
Sarah and Gita.

"We haven't touched it,"
said Sarah.
"We were just going
into the garden, to look for
Mr Gotobed's spectacles.
We'll look for your red feather,
too, Mrs Pitter-Patter."

Mrs Pitter-Patter looked
at Sarah and Gita.

13

"You go with them, Davy, and
keep an eye out for my paint-brush,"
said Mr Puffle.

Sarah, Gita and Davy
went through the gate,
into the garden.

Sarah, Gita and Davy
went into the garden.

The children were looking under
the bushes in the garden, when
they heard a little sound behind them.
They turned round, and
saw the Griffle.
"Are you looking for something?"
the Griffle asked,
in his whiffly-griffly voice.
"We're looking for
Mr Gotobed's spectacles," said Sarah.
"And Mr Puffle's paint-brush,"
said Davy.
"And Mrs Pitter-Patter's red feather,"
said Gita. "They're all lost."

They saw the Griffle.

"I think the Tidy Bird
must be about," said the Griffle.

"What do you mean —
the Tidy Bird?" asked Sarah.

"He tidies everything away
in his nest," said the Griffle.

"What does he look like?"
asked Gita.

"I don't know," said the Griffle.
"He's invisible — you can't see him."

The Griffle said,
''The Tidy Bird must be
in the garden.
You can't see the Tidy Bird.''

"How can we watch
where he goes?"
demanded Sarah.
"He has a little red light
on the top of his head,"
said the Griffle.
"And you can hear him.
He whistles as he flies."
"Let's hide, and wait for him,"
said Sarah.
So they hid behind the hollow tree,
and waited.

Davy and Sarah,
the Griffle and Gita,
all hid.

They hadn't been waiting long,
when they heard a soft
whistling sound.

"Listen!" whispered the Griffle.
"Here he comes."
They saw a little red light
moving through the air.

The Tidy Bird flew
into the garden.

As they watched, the Tidy Bird
dropped down behind a bush.
When he flew up again,
he was carrying a ball.
(They couldn't see the Tidy Bird,
but they could see the ball
as it flew through the air.)

"That's **my** ball," whispered Sarah.
"I lost it in the garden."

Sarah saw her ball.

The little red light and the golden ball
flew towards a tree.
The children and the Griffle followed.

"There's a big nest in the tree!"
whispered Davy.
The Tidy Bird must have heard him,
for the whistling suddenly stopped.
The red light vanished.

"He's gone," said the Griffle.

The Tidy Bird flew
to a tree.

Sarah, Gita and Davy
all ran to the tree, and
looked into the nest.

"Here's my ball," cried Sarah,
picking it up. "And here
are Mr Gotobed's spectacles!"

"Look! Mrs Pitter-Patter's red feather!"
said Gita.
She took it out of the nest.

Davy, Sarah and Gita
looked in the nest.

"And here's Mr Puffle's paint-brush!"
cried Davy. "We must take it to him.
He's going to paint his back door."

"We'll come back and play, Griffle,"
said Sarah. "Please don't go away.
But we must take these things
back to Puddle Lane first."

"We must go back
to Puddle Lane,"
said Sarah.

"We've found them!" cried Sarah.

"We've found them!" cried Gita,
as Davy pulled open the gate,
and they ran into Puddle Lane.
Mr Puffle and Mrs Pitter-Patter
were still there, talking to
Mr Gotobed.

"Here's the paint-brush,"
said Davy.

"However did my paint-brush
get into that garden?"
exclaimed Mr Puffle.

"I can guess," said Mrs Pitter-Patter.

They ran back
into Puddle Lane.

"The Tidy Bird took it," said Sarah.
"He takes all kinds of things, and
tidies them away."

"Nonsense!" said Mrs Pitter-Patter,
snatching the red feather, and
putting it in her hat.
"Don't take my feather again!
Play with your toys, and
leave my feather alone!"

"We didn't take the feather,"
said Sarah. "We found it
in the Tidy Bird's nest."

Mrs Pitter-Patter put
the red feather
in her hat.

Mrs Pitter-Patter only tossed her head, and went off down the lane.

"Thank you, Sarah," said Mr Gotobed. "I'm glad to have my spectacles."

"And I'm glad to have my paint-brush back," said Mr Puffle, as Davy handed it to him. "I've a lot to do today."

Mrs Pitter-Patter
went off,
down the lane.

"Listen!" said Gita. "The Tidy Bird!"
As they all stood listening,
the Tidy Bird came flying
out of the garden.
They saw his little red light
flying down the lane.
He was flying after
Mrs Pitter-Patter.

The Tidy Bird
flew down the lane.

As they stood there, watching,
the Tidy Bird pulled the red feather
out of Mrs Pitter-Patter's hat,
and flew away with it,
up the lane and into the garden.
Mrs Pitter-Patter didn't know
that anything had happened.
She went into her house,
and banged the door.

The Tidy Bird flew away
with the red feather.

"So that was the Tidy Bird!"
said Mr Puffle. "You'll have
to look for that feather
all over again."
He went off down the lane, laughing.

"Dear me!" said Mr Gotobed.
"I must make sure
he doesn't take my spectacles!"
He went back into his house.

"Let's go back to the Griffle,"
said Davy.
And the children went back
into the garden.

Gita, Davy and Sarah
went back to the Griffle.

Notes for the parent/teacher

Turn back to the beginning, and print the child's name in the space on the title page, using ordinary, not capital letters.

Now go through the book again. Look at each picture and talk about it. Point to the caption below, and read it aloud yourself.

Run your finger along under the words as you read, so that the child learns that reading goes from left to right.

Encourage the child to read the words under the illustrations. Don't rush in with the word before he/she has had time to think, but don't leave him/her struggling too long.

Read this story as often as the child likes hearing it. The more opportunities he/she has of looking at the illustrations and **reading** the captions with you, the more he/she will come to recognise the words.

If you have several books, let the child choose which story he/she would like.